© 1994

School Zone Publishing
Grand Haven, MI

Library of Congress Cataloging-in-Publication Data

Bergren, Melissa.
Big, Big Trucks / written and illustrated by Melissa Bergren.

Summary: This book asks questions and gives answers about
various trucks, including fire trucks, tank trucks and toy
trucks.

ISBN: 0-88743-431-2 (paper)
1. Trucks - questions and answers.
2. Easy reading.

CIP Data prepared by Medialog, Inc.

BIG, BIG TRUCKS

WRITTEN AND ILLUSTRATED BY
MELISSA BERGREN

What is red
and shines so bright
as it hurries to fires
day and night?

A Fire Truck

What has arms of steel
that can pick up a tree
and dig a hole
where its new home will be?

A Tree Truck

9

What pours cement
first soft and thick
later to dry
hard as a brick?

A Cement Truck

What is filled to the top
with piles in a lump
of all the things
we need to dump?

A Dump Truck

What goes down streets
on hot summer days
bringing ice-cold treats
while its music plays?

An Ice Cream Truck

What stops at farms
along the way
so that we may have milk
to drink each day?

A Tank Truck

What takes plastic, glass,
and tin cans too
so they may be recycled
into something we can use?

A Recycling Truck

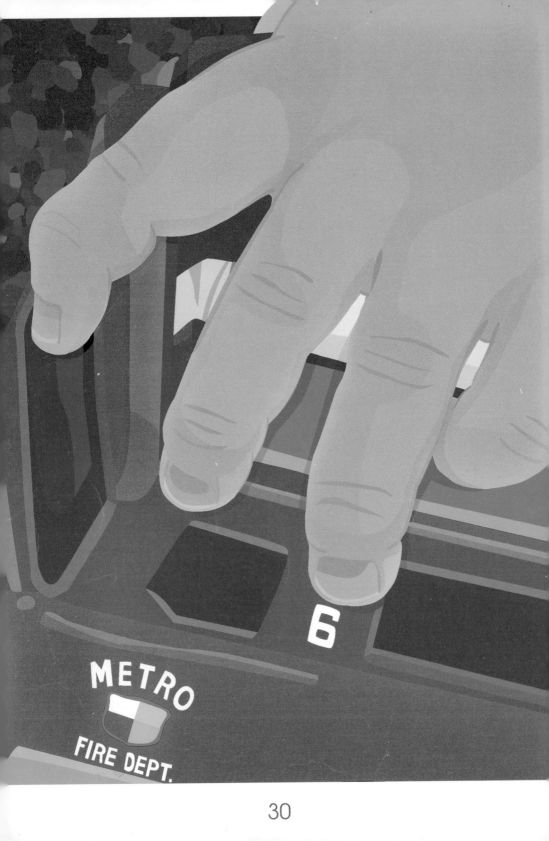

What goes up hills
with a push of the hand
over sticks and stones
and through soft sand?

Toy Trucks